SUPERFUDGE
and the
Garden Ghosts

Pat Thomson
Illustrated by Mike Gordon

Collins
An imprint of HarperCollins*Publishers*

First published in Great Britain by Collins in 1999
Collins is an imprint of HarperCollins*Publishers* Ltd
77-85 Fulham Palace Road, Hammersmith, London, W6 8JB

1 3 5 7 9 8 6 4 2

Text copyright Pat Thomson © 1999
Illustrations copyright Mike Gordon © 1999

ISBN 0 00 675383 3

The author and illustrator assert the moral right to be identified as the
author and illustrator of the work.

Printed and bound in Great Britain by Caledonian International Book
Manufacturing Ltd, Glasgow G64

CONTENTS

SUPERPOOCH AND CHAMPION CHARLIE

Chapter 1

This is a little house in the little town of Wittering. Nothing ever happens here.

Maybe, maybe not.

This is Poochie.

He is Mrs May's little dog. There is nothing interesting about such a sleepy pooch.

Maybe, maybe not.

This is Chatwin the cat.

Chatwin goes everywhere and knows everything. She knows a secret about Poochie.

Mrs May thinks Poochie is her darling little doggie. Chatwin knows that when there is danger, he can become something very different. Bad people had better look out, or **BONES AND BISCUITS** they will have to deal with **SUPERPOOCH!**

One day Mrs May was reading the newspaper. "Poor Charlie bunny," she sighed. "Poor Jack. He worships that rabbit."

Poochie padded over to the table and looked at the newspaper.

THE WITTERING NEWS

JUNIOR CHAMPION STOLEN

Prize-winning rabbit, Charlie, was stolen last night, just one day after becoming Junior Champion. His owner, Jack Burrow, was fast asleep when the crime happened. This morning, the little lad said sadly, "Where is my prize rabbit? Can you help to find Champion Charlie?

"Come along Poochie," said Mrs May.
"I must go and comfort poor Jack."
Poochie trotted along behind her.
He noticed Chatwin was shadowing
them. She slipped behind hedges
and over walls.

Soon they arrived at Jack's house.
Mrs May rang the doorbell and
Jack opened the door immediately.
When he saw Mrs May, he cried,
"Oh Gran, we've lost Charlie!"

"I know. Let's go inside," Mrs May
said, kindly. "I'm going to make a
nice cup of tea. I've brought some
chocolate biscuits."

Poochie sat down on the ground.
He was waiting for Chatwin.

Chapter 2

As soon as Poochie was alone, Chatwin
slid out from under a bush.

"Have you heard the news?"
asked Poochie.

Chatwin nodded. "Bless my little
white socks," she answered.

"Everyone is talking about it. The big grey cat from number twenty-three saw something. He said there was somcone in this garden late last night."

"Did he see any cars?"

"No. Just one person. He was creeping through the garden. The big grey cat thinks it was a man."

"No car." Poochie was thinking aloud. "It is probably someone who lives in Wittering, then."

"Who knows that Charlie is worth a lot of money?" asked Chatwin.

"Only the people who heard Jack talk about the prize yesterday."

"So who did he talk to?"

Poochie stood up and stretched. "I need to run my memory banks. I'll probably need laser vision to search the garden, too. Excuse me one moment."

Chatwin watched as Poochie trotted out of the gate. He was heading for the nearest lamppost. Chatwin closed her eyes.

Chapter 3

"BONES AND BISCUITS!"
A rushing sound filled the air.
Chatwin opened her eyes. Sleepy
Poochie had changed. In his place
stood a large, strong dog. He
looked ready for anything.

"Let's start with my memory banks," said Superpooch. "Jack was out with Mrs May most of yesterday. They were planning his birthday treat.

"First, they went to the toy shop to choose a present. Jack told the assistant there that Charlie had won the prize, but no one else.

"Then on they went through the park. Jack met his friend Sophie and whispered his news to her. My super ears heard everything.

"Then they went to the Hotel Big
to arrange Jack's party. He talked
about everything quite loudly to
Mrs May while they were waiting.

"Later, they went to the pet shop to buy food for Charlie. He blurted out the good news to the shopkeeper and the place was full of people. Anyone could have heard."

"There are plenty of suspects, then," said Chatwin.

"I'm afraid so. We'd better search the garden for clues."

Superpooch began to use his super nose. He started at the gate.

Then he stepped off the path. He followed the trail across the lawn.

It stopped at a window. Under the window was a flower bed.

"Look, a footprint!" said Chatwin.

"Yes," murmured Superpooch. "A *large* footprint."

Then he pounced. "A button!"

His laser eyes had seen a button under a rose bush.

Chatwin looked at it carefully. "It looks like a button from a uniform," she said. "Could it belong to a soldier?"

"I know just where it comes from," said Superpooch.

At that moment, Mrs May and Jack came out. Chatwin hid.

Superpooch pretended to dig furiously.

"Oh dear," said Mrs May. "Bad Poochie has been digging up your garden."

"Look at this," said Jack. He bent down and studied the footprint.

Then he snatched up the button.
"And look at this! It must be a
button from the thief's jacket."

They both stared at it.

"It's not much use though, is it?"
sighed Mrs May. "One button looks
very much like another."

Poochie sighed. He knew exactly where the button came from. His sharp eyes had recognised it. His super nose had smelt something familiar. Humans were no use at all.

Later, he talked to Chatwin about it. "That button comes off the uniform they wear at the Hotel Big. I'll be there tomorrow for the party. Can you come too?"

"I could sneak in over the back wall," said Chatwin.

"You keep them busy downstairs.
I want to search upstairs," said
Poochie.

"Look for me in the dining room,"
said Chatwin. She grinned. "I know
just what to do."

Chapter 4

The next afternoon, Mrs May got ready to go to the Hotel Big. Poochie stayed near to her. He whined.

"Don't worry, my baby," cooed Mrs May. "Mummy won't go without her Poochie-woochie."

Jack was waiting for them at the
hotel. Poochie slid under Mrs May's
chair. He kept very still. Jack's
friends began to arrive, and soon
Poochie was forgotten.

They were halfway through the
party when something happened.

"Get that animal out of here!" yelled a voice in the corridor.

Everyone jumped. A cat streaked into the room. Several waiters ran in after the cat. All the children joined in the chase.

"Keep calm!" yelled the head waiter, pouring tea into a vase of flowers.

The cat tried to get under a table,
but a waiter grabbed hold of her.
The cat dug her claws into the
tablecloth. When the waiter lifted
her up, the tablecloth came too.

It snowed sandwiches. It rained
chocolate biscuits and cream cakes.

"Well done, Chatwin," smiled
Poochie. He slipped out of the room.
He was on the trail.

Chapter 5

Poochie padded swiftly up the stairs.
He moved silently on the thick
carpet. On the landing, he paused
beside a large lamp.

"BONES AND BISCUITS!" he cried. The fringe on the lampshade swung in the rush of air.

He ran on. He found a back staircase. His claws clattered on the bare floorboards.

At the top, he found a row of rooms. He trained his laser eyes on each door. He came to one without a number. He sniffed. There was something behind the door. The room was full of brooms and buckets.

Then Superpooch saw something else. Someone was in the room!

A man was bending over a box. As Superpooch watched, the man lifted out a beautiful rabbit. It was Charlie.

Superpooch waited.

The door opened. A man came out, carrying Charlie. It was one of the waiters from the Hotel Big.

Superpooch crouched and growled softly.

"Get out," snarled the man. He tried to kick Superpooch!

Superpooch seemed to grow. The
hair on his back rose. The narrow
corridor seemed full of Superpooch.

"Stay there." The man was
nervous.

Superpooch moved forward. He
was growling all the time.

The man backed down the stairs.
He was staring into Superpooch's
laser eyes. He had forgotten he was
holding Charlie.

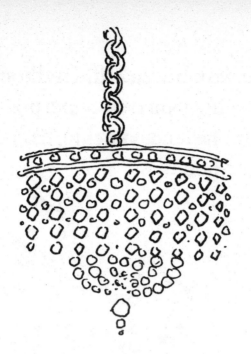

He backed all the way down
the stairs to the room where the
party was.

Jack was just about to cut his
birthday cake, when he looked up.
"It's Charlie!" he yelled.

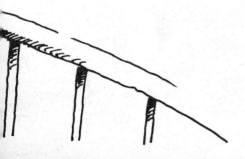

The waiter blinked. He shook his head. He seemed to wake up.

"Yes," he said, quickly. "I found him for you."

But Mrs May and Jack were looking at his uniform.

One pair of buttons.
Another pair of buttons.
And one button and a loose thread.
One button was missing!

Chapter 6

"So what happened next?" asked Chatwin.

It was later that night. She and Poochie were sitting near the lamppost outside Jack's house.

"The vet was called for Charlie. The police were called for the waiter."

"And Charlie is all right," purred Chatwin, "but the waiter is not."

She washed her paws. She was very pleased with herself.

"Exactly," said Poochie, standing up. "Champion Charlie is now snuggled up in his hutch. The waiter is locked up in a police cell."

"The best part was when Charlie was rescued." Chatwin flicked her tail. "But I liked another part, too."

"Which part?" asked Poochie.

"When my claws got caught in the tablecloth. I *did* enjoy that."

Poochie laughed. He trotted towards the lamppost. "Time to go home," he said.

"BONES AND BISCUITS!"

Chatwin waved her tail as her friend zoomed up into the sky. "On the other hand," she said to herself, "perhaps the best thing of all is **SUPERPOOCH!**"

SUPERPOOCH AND THE GARDEN GHOSTS

Chapter 1

This is Mrs May's house in Wittering.
Everything is quiet.

This is her little dog, Poochie.
He is fast asleep.
Maybe, maybe not.

This is Chatwin the cat. She is
wide awake. She prowls the streets.
Will she see something tonight?
Something she needs to tell
SUPERPOOCH about?

Maybe, maybe not.

Chatwin went down to the river. She followed the path, padding along softly. There was no sound. The stars were bright. All was peaceful.

But what was that? Music? Chatwin stopped and listened.

The noise was coming from a boat. Chatwin was puzzled. The boat was not used, except at weekends. She looked through the window.

In the cabin, a light flickered. The television was on. Sitting in front of it were the rotten river rats! They were watching a film.

Chatwin stared. On the screen, a King was walking in a beautiful garden. People were bowing down to him.

"Excellent!" shouted the Boss rat. "I like it!"

The King in the film walked past
a fountain. He walked between
statues of lovely ladies. The ladies
were all wearing flowing dresses.
Then the King waved.

All the rats waved back!
"How strange!" thought Chatwin.
"I've never seen the rats so quiet."
She shook her head and padded on.

Chapter 2

"What a shame!" cried Mrs May.

"It's awful," said Jack and Sophie.

Poochie sighed. He sat down. He
was supposed to be going for a
walk. The other three, however,
were far too busy talking.

"I think there are ghosts in the school garden," said Jack.

"It does seem odd," Sophie agreed. "On Monday, the flower beds were spoilt. Lots of flower heads were missing."

"Just the heads? That's silly," replied Mrs May.

"On Tuesday, the watering can had gone," continued Jack.

"Even though the gates were locked," Sophie reminded him.

"Today, all the garden gnomes have gone."

"What next?" asked Mrs May. "Whatever will go next?"

Forgetting about Poochie, they went indoors.

"Shall I get my walk today?" Poochie wondered. "Maybe, maybe not."

"Bless my little white socks," said another voice. It was Chatwin. She was sitting on the garden wall. "What was all that about?"

Just then, the door opened again. Mrs May and the children were coming back.

"We'll talk tonight," whispered Poochie.

"Poochie-woochie!" cried Mrs May. Did mummy forget her baby's walkies?"

"So long, Babykins," laughed Chatwin and jumped off the wall.

Chapter 3

That night, Chatwin walked along slowly. She was going to Mrs May's house.

First, she stopped at a few dustbins. She found a nice chicken leg. Then she heard something.

"BONES AND BISCUITS!"

She looked up. Something swooped past her. Something flashed away. Her chicken leg had gone!

She ran quickly to Mrs May's house. There was Poochie, under the lamppost.

"Do you want this chicken leg?" he asked.

"I knew it was you," said Chatwin. "Do that again and I'll call you Babykins all the time."

Poochie laughed. "There's been another problem at the school," he said. "Tonight, Jack and Sophie were looking over the school fence at the garden when a rose bush suddenly disappeared – *downwards*!"

"*Downwards*?" Chatwin could not believe her furry ears. "Bless my little white socks!"

"Now they are certain that the garden is haunted."

"So am I," said Chatwin.

"Don't be silly," said Poochie.

"Who makes tunnels under the earth? Who steals things? Who are really rotten?"

"The river rats!" gasped Chatwin.

"Wait a minute. The film. There was a garden in the film." She told Poochie what she had seen by the river.

"My walk was very short today," said Poochie. "Let's go for a walk now. Let's go down to the river."

Chapter 4

Poochie and Chatwin trotted along together. They came to the river path. The moon was shining on the water.

"There's the boat," said Chatwin.

They stepped aboard. The boat swung gently.

"Not a sound," whispered Poochie.

"Where are they?" asked Chatwin.

"I need my laser eyes," said Poochie. "I need my super ears. My super nose will be useful, too. Let's go back to the path!"

They jumped off the boat. Poochie ran to the nearest lamppost. Chatwin saw his shadow on the path.

"BONES AND BISCUITS!"

Chatwin's fur ruffled. The boat rocked a little. The shadow on the path had grown.

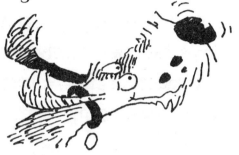

It was **SUPERPOOCH**. He was already sniffing the air.

"We must go behind the boathouse," he called. "Wait a minute. I can hear singing."

"It must be them," said Chatwin.

They both ran behind the boathouse. There were lots of bushes there.

Superpooch looked through the bushes with his laser eyes.

"There's an open space in the middle," he said. Then he started to laugh. "Listen," he said.

We're the rotten river rats,
Our king's the one with the fancy hat.
Forget palaces, castles, and the rest,
Our royal garden is the best.

Chatwin wriggled through the bushes. She came out in the middle and hid herself from the rats. Then she started to laugh, too.

Chapter 5

It was just like the film. At least, it was *almost* like the film.

The Boss rat stood in the middle. He was smiling and waving. On his head was an old bird's nest. It had flowers stuck in it.

Flower heads were stuck in the ground. There was a rose bush. It was leaning sideways. The rats were not very good gardeners.

The Boss rat walked forward. He walked down an avenue of statues. But they were not statues of lovely ladies – they were garden gnomes. One had a wheelbarrow. One had a fishing line. Another had a large sunflower.

The Boss rat stopped. "You must all bow," he said, crossly. Then he smiled again. He continued walking.

"The fountain," he called. "I must have my fountain."

Two rats were standing on an old fish box. They were holding the watering can. As the 'King' walked by, they began to pour water from it. They were very nervous and some splashed on the Boss.

"Not on me, you idiots!" shouted the Boss rat.

"Sorry, Boss. Sorry."

"Your Majesty, if you please."

"Yes, Boss. Yes, Your Majesty," the rats cried.

Chatwin giggled to herself.

The Boss rat stopped by the gnome with the wheelbarrow. He sat in the wheelbarrow.

"Gather round my throne," he said.

He stood up in the wheelbarrow.
"From now on, I shall be really
royal. Very kingly."

He gave a royal wave. The
wheelbarrow tipped over and the
Boss rat fell onto the ground.

Chatwin roared with laughter.
She forgot she was supposed to be
quiet. She forgot she was supposed to
be hidden.

"Who is that?" shouted the Boss
rat. He struggled to his feet. "Find
them! Take them prisoner."

Chapter 6

Poor Chatwin was captured and dragged forward. One rat held each ear. Two rats held each leg. Three rats held her tail.

"You laughed at me," spluttered the Boss rat. "How dare you!"

"You looked very silly," said Chatwin.

This was true, but the Boss rat did not like it.

"You shall be punished!" he shouted. "For that you shall receive one hundred nips."

Chatwin looked round. Suddenly, she saw nothing but rats. They all seemed to have very large teeth.

Then...

"BONES AND BISCUITS!"

A rushing sound filled the air. A huge shape zoomed down into the middle of the circle. It was…

SUPERPOOCH!

The rats squealed and squeaked. They ran in all directions.

"Come back, you cowards," shouted the Boss rat.

But the rats all tried to hide behind the gnomes. No one wanted to meet Superpooch.

Chatwin got up. She looked ruffled. "Wait till I get my paws on that Boss rat," she said.

"He's hiding in the watering can," answered Superpooch.

"No I'm not." The Boss rat's voice sounded all tinny.

Chatwin stood on one side of the
can. Superpooch stood on the other.

"Someone stole the watering can,"
said Superpooch.

"Wasn't me," said the Boss rat,
from inside the can.

"Someone stole the flowers," said
Superpooch.

"Wasn't me," said the Boss rat.

"Someone stole the garden gnomes."

"Wasn't me," said the Boss rat.

"Fibber!" said a little rat.

All the other rats gasped.

"Wasn't, wasn't, wasn't," said the Boss rat, sulkily.

"Well," said Superpooch, "I don't expect you approve, then."

"No, I don't. Disgraceful. Shocking thing to do." The Boss rat peeped over the rim of the can. He glared round.

Superpooch put his paw on the can. "What are you going to do now?"

"Take everything back," said the little rat.

"Be quiet!" shouted the Boss rat. He turned to Superpooch. "These rats have been very bad. They must take everything back at once."

"Excellent, Your Majesty," smiled Superpooch.

Chatwin and Poochie walked home together. They were laughing.

"Jack and Sophie will have another surprise tomorrow," said Chatwin.

"Everything is back in place now."

"Yes," said Poochie, "but some of the gnomes are upside down."

"The rats are not very clever!" giggled Chatwin. "They've put them standing on their heads."

"Now it's time for bed," said Poochie. They were passing a lamppost.

"BONES AND BISCUITS!"
Superpooch zoomed into the air.
"Goodnight, Queen Chatwin," he
called. "Goodnight, my friend."

Chatwin purred. "I shall go to the
school tomorrow. I will sit on the
wall and watch," she said. "They
will be so puzzled. But they will
never know what I know. The
mystery of the garden ghosts was
solved by **SUPERPOOCH!**"